PROPERTY OF:
A-60

INSIGHTS

INSIGHT EDITIONS

San Rafael, California

www.insighteditions.com

LICENSED BLIZZARD ENTERTAINMENT PRODUCT

10 9 8 7 6 5 4 3 2 1